Big Al's
Journey Through
The Yellowhammer State

Aimee Aryal

Illustrated by Gabhor Utomo

MASCOT BOOKS®

www.mascotbooks.com

Tuscaloosa, Alabama is the proud home of the University of Alabama.

Big Al was enjoying a relaxing summer on the campus of the University of Alabama. With football season fast approaching, Big Al decided to take one last summer vacation. He thought it would be great fun to journey throughout The Yellowhammer State, where he could see many interesting places and make new friends along the way.

Before leaving campus, Big Al strolled past Denny Chimes. Bama fans waved to him and yelled, "Hello, Big Al! Roll Tide!"

On his way out of Tuscaloosa, the mascot stopped at the Paul W. Bryant Museum for inspiration. He saw more friends, and they all wished him well. "Enjoy your trip, Big Al!"

From 1948 to 1988 Legion Field hosted the annual Alabama vs. Auburn football game nicknamed the "Iron Bowl."

Big Al made the short drive to Birmingham, where he stopped at historic Legion Field, the site of so many exciting Alabama football games. Outside the stadium, fans noticed the mascot and called, "Hello, Big Al!"

After visiting the stadium, Big Al dressed up in a tuxedo and led the Alabama Symphony Orchestra. The crowd cheered, "Bravo, Big Al!"

Ready to pick up the beat, Big Al broke out his electric guitar and performed at City Stages, Birmingham's famous music festival.
"Rock on, Big Al!" roared his fans.

Finally, he stopped at Vulcan Park and admired the statue with a young friend who said, "Roll Tide, Big Al!"

Standing 56 feet tall and weighing over 100,000 pounds, Birmingham's Vulcan Statue is the largest cast iron statue in the world.

Located along the Tennessee River, Huntsville is known as "Rocket City" and is the home to the United States Space and Rocket Center.

Big Al headed north to Huntsville. He strolled through Big Spring Park and enjoyed fabulous views of the city. Standing on the Japanese Bridge, Big Al spotted ducks, fish, and of course, more Alabama fans. The people nearby were thrilled to see him and called out, "Hello, Big Al! Roll Tide!"

Big Al's next stop was Rocket Park. He met a very smart scientist there who gave him a tour and told the mascot all about rockets and space travel. When Big Al thanked him for being a great tour guide, the scientist smiled and said, "Roll Tide, Big Al!"

Big Al enjoyed spending time in the great outdoors, so he headed off to Lake Guntersville State Park. He went bass fishing and quickly caught a big one! The fish said in a worried voice, "Hello, Big Al!"

Big Al also went sailing. It was so peaceful on the lake. Finally, he rode his jet ski and saw some Crimson Tide fans. The fans waved to Big Al and shouted, "Roll Tide!"

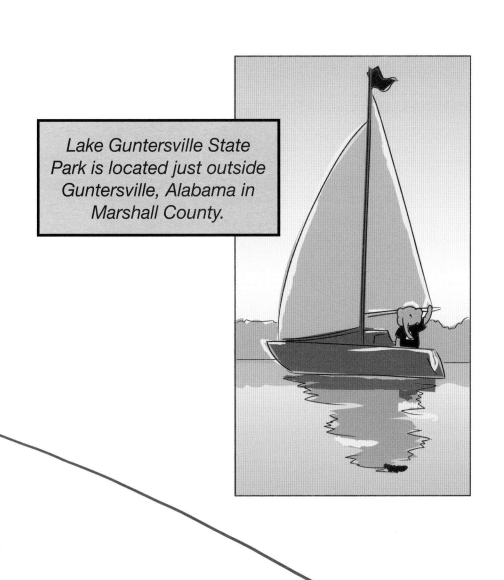

Lake Guntersville State Park is located just outside Guntersville, Alabama in Marshall County.

Anniston is located in Calhoun County, Alabama.

After exercising his body, Big Al was ready to exercise his mind. At the Anniston Museum of Natural History, he came across a family of Alabama fans. They sure were happy to see Big Al! As they walked by, they said, "Hello, Big Al!"

Inside the museum, Big Al joined an archaeologist and the two checked out the mummy exhibit. "Those mummies sure are old," Big Al thought. Next, he went off to see the African savannah exhibit, and got a glimpse of his favorite animal – an elephant!

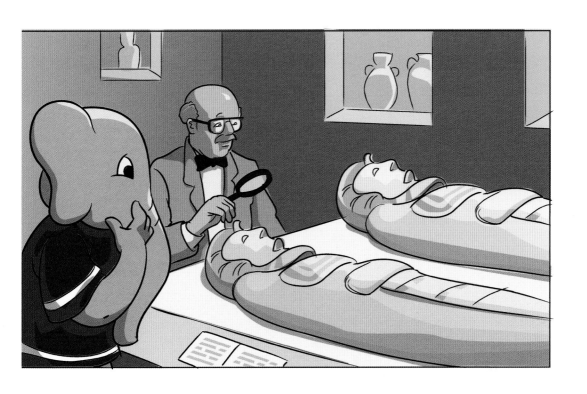

The racetrack at Talladega is over 2 ½ miles long, with capacity for over 175,000 race fans.

Big Al was enjoying his leisurely drive throughout The Yellowhammer State. However, he was ready to pick up the pace. At the world famous Talladega Superspeedway, Big Al took a victory lap around the track! As he passed by the crowded stands, race fans yelled, "Roll Tide!"

When the race began, Big Al joined a pit crew and provided a helping hand. Afterward, Big Al joined a friendly tailgate party, where he enjoyed good food and great company. Some of Big Al's new friends took him to the nearby International Motorsports Hall of Fame & Museum, where he learned about the sport's great history.

Big Al couldn't resist driving over to Auburn! Being on the campus of Auburn University made Big Al feel a little uneasy. Although he tried, it was difficult for the elephant mascot to go unnoticed in Tiger territory. Fortunately, as he walked by Samford Hall, he saw a fellow Alabama fan. The fan smiled and whispered, "Roll Tide, Big Al."

The Alabama State Capitol was completed in 1851.

Happy to leave Auburn behind, Big Al's next stop was Montgomery, the capital of The Yellowhammer State. He was impressed at the size of the Alabama State Capitol. He saw a police officer on the steps who waved and called, "Hello, Big Al! Roll Tide!"

He then went to the Montgomery Zoo, where he saw many different animals, including zebras. "Look, Big Al, they look like referees!" said one of his young friends.

Big Al also visited Shakespeare Gardens, where he performed with the other actors. After a splendid performance, the crowd cheered, "Bravo, Big Al!"

Old Alabama Town is a collection of restored 19th-century buildings in Montgomery, Alabama.

Big Al traveled on to Old Alabama Town, where life was still like it was in the 19th century. Big Al put on the clothes of the time and strolled through the village. Big Al was amazed by how much daily life had changed!

Big Al stopped by one of the factories in Old Alabama Town, where he saw an old cotton gin weaving the crops into clothing. Big Al asked the worker if he could make him a crimson colored shirt. The worker smiled and said, "Roll Tide, Big Al!"

Big Al was ready for a round of golf! He traveled to Dothan, and played one of the courses on the famous Robert Trent Jones Golf Trail. Big Al took a swing, but the only thing that went flying was his golf club! "Fore!" yelled his caddy.

After the round of golf, Big Al stopped at a nearby pool to have fun and go swimming with his new friends. As he splashed into the pool, his pals yelled, "Cannonball, Big Al!"

Mobile is on the Gulf of Mexico and is Alabama's only seaport.

Big Al drove south to Mobile, where he visited the USS Alabama Museum in Mobile Bay. From there, it was a short trip to Bellingrath Gardens and Home, where he admired the beautiful flowers. A bee buzzed, "Hello, Big Al!"

Thrilled about being on the Gulf of Mexico, Big Al went to Dauphin Island, where he lounged on the beach, built himself a sandcastle, and played in the water with some Alabama fans. The fans cheered, "Roll Tide!"

Having traveled all over the entire state, Big Al finally made it back to Tuscaloosa and the University of Alabama. What a great vacation it had been! All his fans were thrilled at his return and cheered, "Hello, Big Al! Welcome home!"

At last, back in his own room, Big Al thought about all the interesting places he visited and the great friends he made along the way. He crawled into his own bed and fell fast asleep.

Good night, Big Al!

Big Al's
Journey Through
The Yellowhammer State

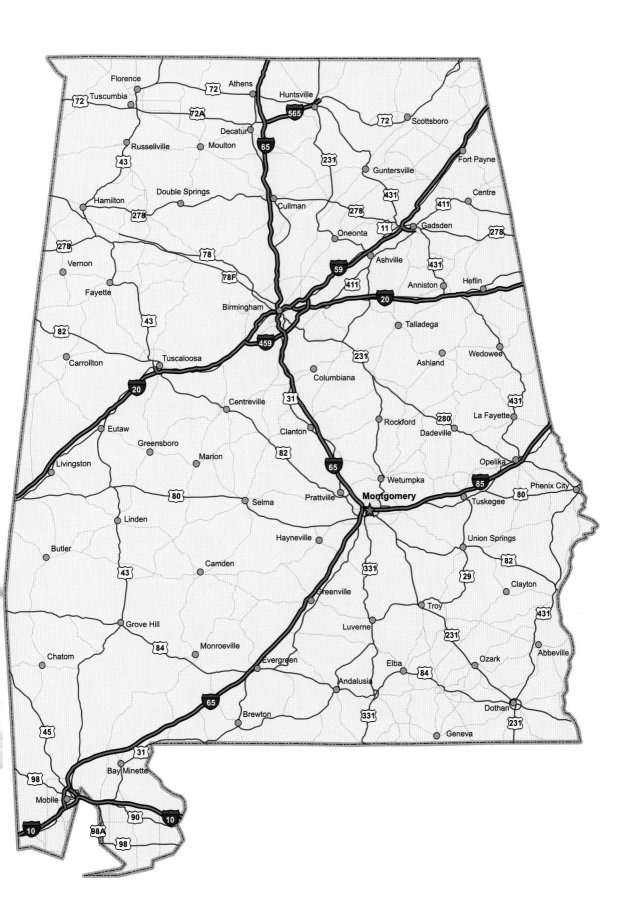

For Anna and Maya. ~ Aimee Aryal

For more information about our products, please visit us online at www.mascotbooks.com.

For more information, please contact Mascot Books,
P.O. Box 220157, Chantilly, VA 20153-0157

BIG AL, UNIVERSITY OF ALABAMA, CRIMSON TIDE,
BAMA, and ROLL TIDE, are trademarks or registered trademarks of
The University of Alabama and are used under license.

ISBN: 978-1-934878-25-5

PRT0610B

Printed in the United States.

www.mascotbooks.com

Title List

Major League Baseball

Team	Title	Author
Boston Red Sox	Hello, *Wally*!	Jerry Remy
Boston Red Sox	*Wally The Green Monster And His Journey Through Red Sox Nation*!	Jerry Remy
Boston Red Sox	Coast to Coast with *Wally The Green Monster*	Jerry Remy
Boston Red Sox	A Season with *Wally The Green Monster*	Jerry Remy
Colorado Rockies	Hello, *Dinger*!	Aimee Aryal
Detroit Tigers	Hello, *Paws*!	Aimee Aryal
New York Yankees	Let's Go, *Yankees*!	Yogi Berra
New York Yankees	*Yankees Town*	Aimee Aryal
New York Mets	Hello, *Mr. Met*!	Rusty Staub
New York Mets	*Mr. Met* and his Journey Through the Big Apple	Aimee Aryal
St. Louis Cardinals	Hello, *Fredbird*!	Ozzie Smith
Philadelphia Phillies	Hello, *Phillie Phanatic*!	Aimee Aryal
Chicago Cubs	Let's Go, *Cubs*!	Aimee Aryal
Chicago White Sox	Let's Go, *White Sox*!	Aimee Aryal
Cleveland Indians	Hello, *Slider*!	Bob Feller
Seattle Mariners	Hello, *Mariner Moose*!	Aimee Aryal
Washington Nationals	Hello, *Screech*!	Aimee Aryal
Milwaukee Brewers	Hello, *Bernie Brewer*!	Aimee Aryal

College

Team	Title	Author
Alabama	Hello, Big Al!	Aimee Aryal
Alabama	Roll Tide!	Ken Stabler
Alabama	Big Al's Journey Through the Yellowhammer State	Aimee Aryal
Arizona	Hello, Wilbur!	Lute Olson
Arkansas	Hello, Big Red!	Aimee Aryal
Arkansas	Big Red's Journey Through the Razorback State	Aimee Aryal
Auburn	Hello, Aubie!	Aimee Aryal
Auburn	War Eagle!	Pat Dye
Auburn	Aubie's Journey Through the Yellowhammer State	Aimee Aryal
Boston College	Hello, Baldwin!	Aimee Aryal
Brigham Young	Hello, Cosmo!	LaVell Edwards
Cal - Berkeley	Hello, Oski!	Aimee Aryal
Clemson	Hello, Tiger!	Aimee Aryal
Clemson	Tiger's Journey Through the Palmetto State	Aimee Aryal
Colorado	Hello, Ralphie!	Aimee Aryal
Connecticut	Hello, Jonathan!	Aimee Aryal
Duke	Hello, Blue Devil!	Aimee Aryal
Florida	Hello, Albert!	Aimee Aryal
Florida State	Let's Go, 'Noles!	Aimee Aryal
Georgia	Hello, Hairy Dawg!	Aimee Aryal
Georgia	How 'Bout Them Dawgs!	Aimee Aryal
Georgia	Hairy Dawg's Journey Through the Peach State	Vince Dooley
Georgia Tech	Hello, Buzz!	Vince Dooley
Gonzaga	Spike, The Gonzaga Bulldog	Aimee Aryal / Mike Pringle
Illinois	Let's Go, Illini!	
Indiana	Let's Go, Hoosiers!	Aimee Aryal
Iowa	Hello, Herky!	Aimee Aryal
Iowa State	Hello, Cy!	Aimee Aryal
James Madison	Hello, Duke Dog!	Amy DeLashmutt
Kansas	Hello, Big Jay!	Aimee Aryal
Kansas State	Hello, Willie!	Aimee Aryal
Kentucky	Hello, Wildcat!	Dan Walter
LSU	Hello, Mike!	Aimee Aryal
LSU	Mike's Journey Through the Bayou State	Aimee Aryal
Maryland	Hello, Testudo!	Aimee Aryal
Michigan	Let's Go, Blue!	Aimee Aryal
Michigan State	Hello, Sparty!	Aimee Aryal
Minnesota	Hello, Goldy!	Aimee Aryal
Mississippi	Hello, Colonel Rebel!	Aimee Aryal
Mississippi State	Hello, Bully!	Aimee Aryal

Pro Football

Team	Title	Author
Carolina Panthers	Let's Go, Panthers!	Aimee Aryal
Chicago Bears	Let's Go, Bears!	Aimee Aryal
Dallas Cowboys	How 'Bout Them Cowboys!	Aimee Aryal
Green Bay Packers	Go, Pack, Go!	Aimee Aryal
Kansas City Chiefs	Let's Go, Chiefs!	Aimee Aryal
Minnesota Vikings	Let's Go, Vikings!	Aimee Aryal
New York Giants	Let's Go, Giants!	Aimee Aryal
New York Jets	J-E-T-S! Jets, Jets, Jets!	Aimee Aryal
New England Patriots	Let's Go, Patriots!	Aimee Aryal
Pittsburgh Steelers	Here We Go Steelers!	Aimee Aryal
Seattle Seahawks	Let's Go, Seahawks!	Aimee Aryal
Washington Redskins	Hail To The Redskins!	Aimee Aryal

Basketball

Team	Title	Author
Dallas Mavericks	Let's Go, Mavs!	Mark Cuban
Boston Celtics	Let's Go, Celtics!	Aimee Aryal

Other

Team	Title	Author
Kentucky Derby	White Diamond Runs For The Roses	Aimee Aryal
Marine Corps Marathon	Run, Miles, Run!	Aimee Aryal

Team	Title	Author
Missouri	Hello, Truman!	Aimee Aryal
Nebraska	Hello, Herbie Husker!	Todd Donoho
North Carolina	Hello, Rameses!	Aimee Aryal
North Carolina	Rameses' Journey Through the Tar Heel State	Aimee Aryal
North Carolina St.	Hello, Mr. Wuf!	Aimee Aryal
North Carolina St.	Mr. Wuf's Journey Through North Carolina	Aimee Aryal
Notre Dame	Let's Go, Irish!	Aimee Aryal
Ohio State	Hello, Brutus!	Aimee Aryal
Ohio State	Brutus' Journey	Aimee Aryal
Oklahoma	Let's Go, Sooners!	Aimee Aryal
Oklahoma State	Hello, Pistol Pete!	Aimee Aryal
Oregon	Go Ducks!	Aimee Aryal
Oregon State	Hello, Benny the Beaver!	Aimee Aryal
Penn State	Hello, Nittany Lion!	Aimee Aryal
Penn State	We Are Penn State!	Joe Paterno
Purdue	Hello, Purdue Pete!	Aimee Aryal
Rutgers	Hello, Scarlet Knight!	Aimee Aryal
South Carolina	Hello, Cocky!	Aimee Aryal
South Carolina	Cocky's Journey Through the Palmetto State	Aimee Aryal
So. California	Hello, Tommy Trojan!	Aimee Aryal
Syracuse	Hello, Otto!	Aimee Aryal
Tennessee	Hello, Smokey!	Aimee Aryal
Tennessee	Smokey's Journey Through the Volunteer State	Aimee Aryal
Texas	Hello, Hook 'Em!	Aimee Aryal
Texas	Hook 'Em's Journey Through the Lone Star State	Aimee Aryal
Texas A & M	Howdy, Reveille!	Aimee Aryal
Texas A & M	Reveille's Journey Through the Lone Star State	Aimee Aryal
Texas Tech	Hello, Masked Rider!	Aimee Aryal
UCLA	Hello, Joe Bruin!	Aimee Aryal
Virginia	Hello, CavMan!	Aimee Aryal
Virginia Tech	Hello, Hokie Bird!	Aimee Aryal
Virginia Tech	Yea, It's Hokie Game Day!	Frank Beamer
Virginia Tech	Hokie Bird's Journey Through Virginia	Aimee Aryal
Wake Forest	Hello, Demon Deacon!	Aimee Aryal
Washington	Hello, Harry the Husky!	Aimee Aryal
Washington State	Hello, Butch!	Aimee Aryal
West Virginia	Hello, Mountaineer!	Aimee Aryal
Wisconsin	Hello, Bucky!	Aimee Aryal
Wisconsin	Bucky's Journey Through the Badger State	Aimee Aryal

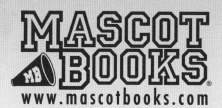

SCHOOL PROGRAM

Promote reading. Build spirit. Raise money.™

Mascot Books® is creating customized children's books for public and private elementary schools all across America. Containing school-specific story lines and illustrations, our books are beloved by principals, librarians, teachers, parents, and of course, by young readers.

Our books feature your mascot taking a tour of your school, while highlighting all the things and events that make your school community such a special place.

The Mascot Books Elementary School Program is an innovative way to promote reading and build spirit, while offering a fresh, new marketing or fundraising opportunity.

Starting Is As Easy As 1-2-3!

1 You tell us all about your school community. What makes your school unique? What are your well-known traditions? Why do parents and students love your school?

2 With the information you share with us, Mascot Books creates a one-of-a-kind hardcover children's book featuring your school and your mascot.

3 Your book is delivered!

Great new fundraising idea for public schools!

Innovative way to market your private school to potential new students!

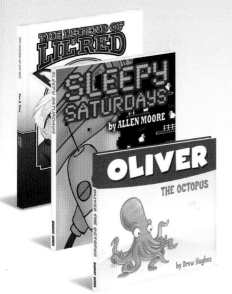

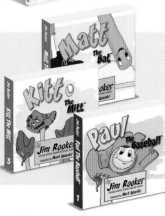